P9-AGM-357

# Mia
## and the Big Sister Ballet

by Robin Farley

pictures by Aleksey and Olga Ivanov

**HARPER**

*An Imprint of HarperCollinsPublishers*

Mia is in the city!
Her dance class
is visiting the theater.

# Mia's sister
# will be there!

Mia's sister is named Ava.

Ava is a dancer!

Mia and her friends
watch Ava onstage.

Ava twirls and leaps.

She is a star!

The curtain closes.

Ava bows.

The class cheers!

Now Ava will show
the class a new dance!

Miss Bird takes the class
up to the stage.

Ava wears

blue toe shoes.

She has on a blue tutu.

"Let's dance!"
Ava says.

Mia watches Ava twirl.

Then Mia twirls.

Mia dances her best.

"Look, Ava!" she says.

But Ava is busy.

She is helping others.

Ava helps Anna point her toes.

Ava helps Ruby bend her legs
into a plié.

Ava helps Bella spring
into the air.

And Ava helps Tess spin
around and around.

But Ava doesn't help Mia.

And Ava doesn't see
Mia dance her best.

Mia is sad.
She sits down
on a bench.

She doesn't feel
like dancing anymore.

Ava sees Mia.
"Why don't you
want to dance?"
Ava asks.

"You were too busy
to watch me," Mia tells her.

"I was helping your friends," Ava tells Mia.

"I already know you're a star!"

Ava gives Mia a big hug!
"Will you dance with me?"
Ava asks.

# The sisters dance together!

When she grows up
Mia is going to be
just like her big sister—
a dancing star!

# Dictionary

## Theater

(you say it like this: the-a-ter)

A building where dancers perform

## Plié

(you say it like this: plee-ay)

A dance position where you

bend at the knees

## Toe Shoes

(you say it like this: tow shooz)

The shoes that ballet dancers wear